Now and Then

Kane Miller
A DIVISION OF EDC PUBLISHING

Contents

Introduction

Picture the world we live in. It's a vast, wide world filled with billions of people all living very different lives. With today's incredible technology, everything seems to move very quickly—we can travel all over the world in superfast airplanes, talk to almost anyone at the push of a button, and even shoot up into space! We have access to seemingly endless resources and entertainment—food, movies, music—often from the comfort of our own warm, dry homes.

Things weren't always so simple, though. In our world's long history, people had to do lots of things very differently. How did people communicate before telephones and the internet? How could you cook your dinner without an oven or a refrigerator? What kind of sports and entertainment did people enjoy fifty years ago—or a hundred, or even a thousand?

Now and Then explores the weird and wonderful lives that people have lived throughout humanity's vast history. Discover what people wore in ancient Greece, attend an ancient Egyptian school, play a wild and dangerous Aztec ball game, and settle in to watch a silent movie in the 1920s—all in amazing technicolor.

Getting Around

Throughout history, humans traveled long and short distances to find food and shelter. Hundreds of thousands of years ago, we walked from place to place on foot, yet as we began to live in permanent settlements, the way we traveled began to change. Today, we can reach the other side of the world in less than two days, a journey that 100 years ago would have been impossible! Astronauts can even launch into space in a rocket... in less than 10 minutes!

On the Road

Once humans began living in communities, around 9,500 years ago, we started farming crops and keeping animals. We traded goods with other villages that had items we needed. To carry them, we used animals, such as horses, to pull carts along early roads. When you travel on busy freeway systems today, imagine how long the journey would have taken before cars were invented in the late 1800s.

Off the Rails

When the first steam train was invented in the early 1800s, people didn't know if it was safe to travel at such high speeds, and even wondered if they would be able to breathe! It was an exciting time—people could visit other cities quickly and easily, and even take vacations. Early trains ran on coal, but today, trains are much faster, quieter, and more energy efficient.

All at Sea

Humans often settled near rivers, which allowed for easy travel, and access to water for farming. Ancient Egyptians flourished along the banks of the River Nile, sailing its waters in boats made from a plant called papyrus. Many cultures sailed the oceans, too. Thousands of years ago, Polynesian people crossed the enormous Pacific Ocean on wooden rafts. Over time, more and more adventurers took to the waves on larger ships, traveling all over the world.

Taking to the Skies

At one time, air travel was thought to be impossible. Yet today, eight million people fly every day! In 1903, the famous Wright brothers first took to the air for 12 seconds. It was a good start! In the 20th century, we saw great advancement, with people battling to be the first to fly across oceans, continents, and even the world. From the 1950s, commercial flights became more and more popular, and today it's possible to fly all over the world in comfort.

Lift Off!

Fancy a trip into space? It's possible! In 1961, the first cosmonaut, Yuri Gagarin, went into orbit. Since then, more than 500 people have exited Earth's atmosphere. Today, people live on the International Space Station all year round, carrying out scientific experiments. We may even see people reach Mars in the 2030s... NASA is working on it. Space vacations are also an (expensive) possibility for the future!

Traveling by road...
Then

The Romans are the most famous road builders of all time. They knew that the fastest way to get from one point to another was by following a straight line, and built roads all over their enormous empire. In towns and cities, Romans moved around using horse-drawn chariots. Imagine what they would have made of the first ever car, invented in 1885 by Karl Benz.

Karl Benz's invention was the first gasoline-fueled vehicle. It could move at speeds of around 6 mph—only a little faster than walking!

Traveling by train...
Then

The first working steam train was built by a British man named Richard Trevithick. This kick-started a new way for people to travel. Passengers were able to relocate with ease, and cover vast distances across difficult terrain. Higher volumes of goods could also be transported, which meant building new towns was far easier.

Early steam trains traveled at around 40 mph. Any faster and they could have flown off the rails completely!

Traveling by road...
Now

Today, more than 70 million cars are produced each year. They can travel much faster than the first automobiles—the fastest can reach 300 mph! Our towns and cities are connected by vast networks of roads, and millions of people drive on them every day.

Cars of the future may be very different! Experts are trying to make them safer and better for the environment. One day, we may all have driverless cars, fueled by electricity.

Traveling by train...
Now

Today, trains can travel through mountains, under cities, and even in specially built tunnels under the sea!

We still use trains daily, and there are many types—from freight trains to inner-city trains for busy workers. The fastest trains today use magnets to move. Maglev trains, in operation in Japan, may one day be mainstream. They can reach super-fast speeds of more than 250 mph.

Communication

Today, we can communicate in so many different ways. In person, we talk and use hand gestures, and if we want to speak to someone on the other side of the world, we can use all kinds of technology, such as text messages and email. Non-verbal people will often use sign language. Long ago, humans left simple cave paintings behind to tell stories and pass on messages. Since then, we've found all kinds of ways to make communication easier.

Picture Perfect

One of the earliest forms of writing was invented by the ancient Egyptians, in around 3200 BCE. Hieroglyphs are an alphabet made up of pictures of animals, symbols, and objects that were used in daily life. Scribes would write them on paper made from papyrus. They were also carved into stone and painted on walls. Other cultures, such as Native Americans and the Inuit people, also developed a system of writing based on pictures.

No Smoke without Fire

Ancient peoples all over the world have used smoke signals and fire beacons to communicate. They would use clouds of smoke to let others know important news. If the message needed to travel a very long distance, often a chain of fire would be lit.

Dots and Dashes

In the 1830s, Samuel Morse invented Morse code—a system of communication that used long and short electrical pulses, called "dots" and "dashes," to send messages along wires. After a cable was laid between the United States and Europe, these "telegrams" made almost-instant cross-continental communication possible! Soon after, the telephone was invented—and this time, sound could flow through wires. Amazing!

Spaced Out

The development of satellites absolutely revolutionized communication. Today, we can send messages to people anywhere in the world in mere seconds. Messages are beamed up into space, then bounced off a satellite to a different location, thousands of miles away!

Getting Smart

Many people own smartphones or tablets, and can use them to send texts, photos, and videos in an instant.

Communicating in the...
Stone Age

Before writing was invented, cave paintings were used to tell stories and leave messages. Archaeologists have discovered paintings from over 35,000 years ago!

Early cave paintings of horses and bulls can be found in the Lascaux Caves in France. They are believed to be up to 20,000 years old.

In the past, specially trained birds called homing pigeons were used to deliver letters! They would fly for miles to bring their cargo to certain locations.

Communicating in the...
16th Century

Before telephones, people would write each other letters and send them by horse or wagon, or even by boat. Sometimes letters took weeks to arrive, and riders were often targeted by robbers, as they were known to carry valuables.

Letters used to be sealed with wax. If the wax was broken, you knew your letter had been read.

Communicating in the...
19th Century

The telephone was patented in the US in 1876 by a Scottish-born inventor named Alexander Graham Bell. It allowed people to talk to each other in real time, across great distances, by sending sound messages down a wire.

The design of telephones has changed a lot. Early phones were nowhere near as sleek. They had a rotary dial, which had to be moved using one finger for each digit of the telephone number.

The first phone calls could cost hundreds of dollars—today we can often talk for free.

Communicating...
Now

Today, people can use video calling software to talk to each other face-to-face, in real time, all the way across the planet.

You can now use filters that change how you look or sound over video calls as well as on photographs.

Being able to send videos across the planet in less than a second would have seemed impossible to people in the past!

Taking Pictures

Today, if something catches our eye, we can take a high-quality photo in an instant using a smartphone. We can also store hundreds of images with ease... but it wasn't always so simple! Before cameras were invented, if someone wanted a portrait they would have to stand still for hours, if not days, while an artist painted them! The first known photograph was taken almost 200 years ago by Joseph Nicéphore Niépce.

Taking Things Seriously

Sometimes, photos can be incredibly important. News photographers travel around the world taking images to record events. We also use photos for formal occasions, such as portraits of important people or leaders. In the past, it took a while for a photo to be taken—it was hard work, which is why many people in old photos aren't smiling.

Having Fun

As well as recording memories, one of the reasons people like to take so many snaps is the chance to have fun and be silly! In the past, photos were printed on film and had to be taken away to be developed. This took time and cost money. Today, we can put a phone into selfie mode and easily take as many pictures as we like!

In the Dark

When photos are printed onto paper, rather than stored digitally on phones or memory cards, they have to be developed. To do this, a darkroom may be used. Although it sounds mysterious, it is simply a workshop lit with a glowing red light. Here, a piece of equipment similar to a projector beams light through the "negative" film from the camera, onto paper, and a photograph is formed.

Wedding Bells

Because photography used to be so expensive and time-consuming, it was usually only used on special occasions, such as weddings. This means we have lots of photos of famous people and big events in the past, but not so many of day-to-day life.

Out of this World

Sometimes it is hard to believe just how far photography has come. Today, huge cameras can take photos of far into space. These lenses show us stars and galaxies millions of miles away. Cameras have allowed us to see farther than many would have ever imagined—and that's awesome! Astronauts frequently send back wonderful images of Earth from the International Space Station, and the first space selfie was taken by astronaut Buzz Aldrin in 1966.

People would surround themselves with their possessions, even pets, to show what kind of person they were.

Renaissance

How times have changed! Today, you can take hundreds of pictures of yourself in seconds. Hundreds of years ago, though, if people wanted a picture of themselves to keep for future generations, they would have to pay for portraits to be painted, or even paint them themselves.

Portraits of wealthy people have existed for as long as there has been art.

Because hiring an artist was expensive, we mostly have portraits of rich people from the past.

Taking pictures...
Now

Today, people easily take photos of everything, from big events and holidays to snaps of food for social media. Picture takers from many walks of life have access to digital cameras, smartphones, and tablets—it's never been quicker or easier.

The Eiffel Tower, in Paris, France, is one of the most photographed places in the world. How romantic!

Selfie sticks have been very popular over the last decade. They allow you to take an image of yourself easily—and they are a lot of fun!

Over 20 billion photographs have been uploaded to Instagram since it was launched!

Clothes

For hundreds of thousands of years, humans have fashioned clothes to protect our bodies from the elements, keeping our skin safe from the hot sun, or warm and dry in the wind and rain. As civilizations developed, we began adorning our bodies with clothes and jewelry to show personal status or rank. Until quite recently, clothes were vastly different from civilization to civilization, depending on the climate, and on the dyes and materials available. But with today's technologies, if you can imagine it, you can wear it!

New Material

Different areas around the world used varying techniques and materials to make fabrics. In Asia, people made delicate silk using a substance produced by silkworms. The soft material became highly sought after and expensive in Western countries. Colder, mountainous countries farmed sheep and llamas specifically for their warm wool. Nowadays, we have machines to create some material for us, but in the past we always had to use our hands.

Dye Hard

Until the 19th century, simple fabrics were colored using natural sources such as plants, insects, and even shellfish! Different dyes used to be rare and expensive to make, so they were often used to express wealth—the color purple, for example, is associated with royalty.

Making Things Up

Today, we can use makeup to express ourselves, cover up blemishes, and even change the shape of our face to make ourselves look different. In the past, it was used in a similar way, but could be highly dangerous—early face powder got its white color from a poison called cyanide, which could make people very sick.

Tall Tales

Nowadays, high heels are mostly worn by women, yet in the 1600s many men wore them to make themselves appear taller. They would also wear tall hats, known as stovepipes, in an attempt to increase their height.

Dressing Up

In many countries during World War II (1939-1945), there was a shortage of material, so clothing was rationed. People had to make do with simple outfits, and make repairs instead of getting new clothes. Once the war ended and people had access to more fabric, fashion turned to big, full skirts.

Clothes...
Through the Ages

Each morning, when we get up and choose an outfit for the day, what we choose to wear depends on many different factors—the weather, our culture, and our own personal style. Nowadays, we have a seemingly endless choice of what to wear, and there are clothes in all sorts of colors, fabrics, and styles. Throughout history, the clothes people wore changed with the fashions and new developments of the day. What do you think people will think of the clothes you wear today in 100 years?

Stone Age, >100,000 years ago

Over 100,000 years ago, in what is now the Middle East, the first clothes were made of animal skin, likely sewn together with bone needles.

Renaissance, 500 years ago

During the Renaissance, more complex fashions arose, with extravagant ruffs and detailed embroidery. Fashions were usually set by royalty and then copied by the middle classes.

Ancient Greece, 2,500 years ago

In ancient Greece, the high price of fabric meant people didn't want to cut it up. Instead, they wore loose robes and togas made from one large piece of material.

Byzantine, 700 years ago

In the Byzantine era, people began to use their clothes to show wealth—rich people wore brighter colors and prints, while poor people wore duller, undyed clothes.

Industrial Revolution, 250 years ago

New technologies meant that clothes could be made far more easily. The invention of machine weaving, dyeing, and sewing lead to clothes being produced cheaply, in bulk, for the first time.

Now

Today, almost anything goes. There is an amazing range of styles and colors available, and much of it can be bought cheaply. Some people still make their own clothes!

Homes

Early humans took shelter in caves and gathered around fires to keep warm. They also built dwellings from mammoth bones and animal hide. As time passed, people around the world began building more permanent places to live, using materials such as mud and wood. Some homes were even built on stilts over water! We have developed many ingenious ways to keep warm, clean, and safe over the years. Today's modern apartments in glassy skyscrapers show how far we've come.

Sweet Dreams

The first beds were simple piles of straw with animal skins on top. In ancient Egypt, people slept on piles of palm leaves, while in ancient Rome they stuffed cloth with reeds. Traditionally, in parts of China, people slept on a platform over a stove to keep warm. Luckily, in the 1800s, the spring mattress was developed, making it much easier to get a good night's sleep!

Keep it Clean

Keeping clean is very important for our health, yet it hasn't always been easy to do. In Elizabethan England, most people would only be bathed twice—once at birth, and once after they died. They had poor hygiene and didn't live as long as we do today. The Romans, however, were famous for their bathing rituals; they would wash regularly together at ornate public baths.

A Sheltered Life

First and foremost, our homes should shelter us from the elements. They are built to withstand different types of weather, depending on whether we live in a hot or cold place. In Neolithic times (the late Stone Age), Icelandic people would put grass on their roofs to keep warm and dry. Today, we use modern materials to insulate our homes and keep us cozy.

Sticking Together

Where does your family spend time together? Is it in the living room, or perhaps the kitchen? People have always lived in groups, for safety and company. Traditionally, people gathered around a fire or hearth to keep warm, tell stories, and eat. Large feasts have been common throughout history, and many people still love coming together for a good meal.

Homes...
Through the Ages

The development of houses is fascinating—it shows how our needs have changed over the centuries. Homes look very different across the world, yet they are all designed to provide us with warmth, safety, and comfort. The most common kinds of houses today are apartments, single-family detached houses, duplexes, row houses, and town houses. The most lavish of all—mansions—may have all kinds of luxuries, such as large home theaters and swimming pools.

In the Stone Age, people sheltered in the mouths of caves—too far in, and it was too dark and cold. At the entrance, they could see their surroundings more clearly, and watch out for dangerous animals.

A thatched roof is made of natural materials, including reeds. This means it has to be replaced every ten years or so, or it will mold. These roofs have been used since Neolithic times.

In the 11th century, houses made from earth and straw were built. Known as cob houses, they lasted for hundreds of years.

Today, we have the engineering skills to build incredible buildings that are hundreds of feet tall. The Burj Khalifa, in Dubai, is 2,716.5 feet tall, making it the tallest building in the world. Other homes can be found in all sorts of weird and wonderful buildings.

Sturdy Victorian houses were built to last—and many still exist today. They were often quite ornate, and showed off how much money the owners had. The Victorian period also saw the invention of the first ever flushing toilet. What a relief!

As populations soared, we began running out of space to build houses. From the late 19th century, we began building tower blocks and towering skyscrapers that allowed lots of people to live comfortably on a relatively small area of land.

Watching movies

Every year, people flock to movie theaters all around the world to watch the latest blockbusters. We can also stream hundreds of films online at home, thanks to the internet. The fascination with movies started over 100 years ago, in the 1880s. That's when the first motion pictures were made. The first public showings were a little later, in the 1890s. Back then, movies were in black-and-white, and were much shorter than the feature-length films we are used to today.

Silence is Golden

It's hard to imagine, but until 1927, movies didn't have any sound! Dialogue would sometimes be shown as subtitles, and a pianist in the theater would play music along with the movie to create an atmosphere.

Wild West

Westerns were once a very popular genre, starting with the 1903 short film *The Great Train Robbery*. They included elaborate stunts long before professionals were hired to act out dangerous shots!

Larger than Life

Today, movie theaters offer 3-D screenings of many films, and 3-D-compatible TVs are for sale in stores. This technology requires special glasses to create the impression that images are coming out of the screen, toward the viewer.

Getting it on Tape

By the 1950s, it was possible to watch movies at home. VCRs came into existence, and people could rent or buy movies from stores. They could even record programs and movies from TV onto tapes to watch again.

Spoiled for Choice

Today, people can stream hundreds of movies at home using subscription sites. It is very popular to watch movies on laptops and tablets—especially while traveling—but many people still love the tradition of going to the movies and savoring the experience. Technology is increasing at a very fast rate—soon, people might be able to enjoy virtual reality films. How futuristic!

Watching movies in...
the 1920s

When movie theaters became mainstream in the early 19th century, films were in black-and-white. Theaters often showed double features (two shorter movies, back-to-back) for the price of one. At first, films were silent, until "talkies" became popular in the late 1920s. Early actors were known for their use of grand gestures and overacting—without sound, they had to make the movies exciting somehow!

One type of early movie theater was called a "nickelodeon." It only cost a nickel to watch films shown there.

Hollywood is the oldest film industry in the world. Its most successful "golden" era was between 1927 and 1948.

People have more choices now than ever before—it's possible to watch hundreds of different movies from your living room.

With tablets and Wi-Fi, movies can be watched almost anywhere.

Watching movies…
Now

Today, dozens of movies are released every single month, and can be watched from the comfort of home. There are lots of streaming services which give us access to hundreds of movies. They can be watched in family groups, with friends, or simply on portable devices as we journey from one place to the next on trains and planes.

Finding food

Humans need to eat food to survive, and it has never been easier for much of the world to find sustenance. Large scale farming, advances in food production, and conveniently placed stores mean a huge variety of food is available to purchase all year round. In the past, people had to hunt, find, or grow their food, which took hours each day and used up a lot of energy, but over thousands of years, the way we get our food has changed.

On the Hunt

Until farming was developed around 10,000 years ago, humans found food by hunting, fishing, and gathering plants and fungi in the wild. People would use rocks, or handmade spears and arrows, to hunt down animals as big as enormous, elephant-like creatures called woolly mammoths. Today, only a few tribes, such as the Hadza in Tanzania, Africa, still live this way. This tribe eats plants, such as baobab fruit, and hunts game animals for meat.

Living off the Land

After people began keeping farm animals and growing crops, life became much simpler. Hunting was no longer necessary, as meat was readily available, and people had access to products such as eggs, wool, and cows' milk, which could be made into butter and cheese. Settlements would also trade goods with other farms and villages.

Loafing Around

Many ancient civilizations, such as the Egyptians and the Greeks, grew grain, which they ground up to make bread, cooking the loaves in brick ovens. In Roman times, bakers were expected to mark every loaf they made with a personalized stamp to prove they were good quality.

Spicing Things Up

As people began to navigate the world, travelers brought back foods from other countries. For example, Spanish explorers brought the potato to Europe from the Americas in the 16th century. Pirates targeted spice ships, making spice trading a dangerous but profitable pursuit—spices such as saffron sold for more money than gold.

Easy as Pie

Today, it's possible to buy food from all over the world in grocery stores, and take it home to cook—or to order ready-cooked food to go. Stocked daily with almost everything imaginable, these large stores include items such as spices, which in the past were too expensive for most people.

Cooking in the...
Stone Age

In the Stone Age, hunter-gatherers moved from place to place, hunting animals to eat with bows, arrows, and spears. They cut raw meat with sharp stones, wrapped it in wet leaves, and cooked it over an open fire. They couldn't store meat easily, so each day they would have to start the search again.

Large fish, such as salmon, were caught by hunters, using clever traps and sharp spears.

Perfectly preserved stone ovens have been found in Pompeii, Italy. Because of this, we know the Romans liked pizza as much as we do!

Cooking in the...
Roman Empire

Ancient Romans ate a wide variety of foods, depending on their wealth. People of all walks of life had access to wine—and plenty of it! Meals often included fresh fruits and vegetables, grains, and meats.

The most elaborate meal of the day for a Roman was dinner, which they called "cena." Food was cooked and served in clay pots.

Cooking in the...
Victorian Era

In Britain, in the Victorian era (1837-1901), there was a large divide between the rich and poor. The wealthy had their meals cooked by full-time kitchen staff who made elaborate meals every day for the family. Cooks and kitchen maids usually lived with the family they worked for, often sleeping in the kitchen by the oven, and would eat the leftovers from the family's meals.

Shelf-stable products, such as condensed milk and dried eggs, became available in the Victorian era.

Railways made it possible to carry food long distances to denser populations in growing cities.

Cooking...
Now

Nowadays, cooking is easier than ever. People can store food for a long time in cold refrigerators and freezers, rather than having to find fresh food every day. Food can be cooked super quickly in convenient ovens and microwaves.

All kinds of amazing appliances are available to help today's cook. Ice cream, coffee, and bread can be made at the touch of a button!

A huge variety of different foods and recipes are available. Today, if you can think of it, you can probably cook it.

Many people choose to be vegetarian, meaning they don't eat meat, or vegan, meaning they avoid all animal products, including eggs and milk.

Sports

Ancient records of sports have been found from over 3,000 years ago, and humans have always engaged in some form of movement or exercise. (It was important when people needed to be fit enough to hunt.) The earliest sports often involved training for war, including practicing throwing spears and rocks. Nowadays, sports is a massive industry—many people play professionally, while others simply play sports for fun and to stay healthy.

Fighting Dirty

Wrestling is the oldest sport of all. It is depicted in ancient Sumerian poetry (from modern-day Iraq) from around 2000 BCE, and it became part of the ancient Greek Olympics in 708 BCE. Still popular today, it features in many different cultures worldwide.

Having a Ball

The Mesoamerican ball game was an exciting yet dangerous sport... that could end in death! It was often played by warriors, and the losers could be sacrificed to the gods. This early team sport was a little like basketball, and started around 1400 BCE. The aim was to knock a hard, rubber ball through tiny, stone hoops several feet up in the air. The catch—you couldn't use your hands or feet, so had to hit the ball using your elbows, knees, and hips.

A Hard Day's Knight

In the 1300s, knights and nobles took part in the popular sport of jousting. Two people tried to knock each other off their horses using long lances. It drew huge crowds and the knights were treated like rock stars! They could win money, titles, and even the favor of important ladies.

It's not Cricket

England's national sport is cricket, a bat-and-ball game that's been played throughout the British Empire since the 13th century. Today, it is hugely popular in many areas of the world that were once colonized by Britain, including India, Australia, New Zealand, and Sri Lanka. Every year, England and Australia compete in a cricket tournament called the Ashes.

International Success

Today, sports are still incredibly popular, with huge international tournaments enjoyed by millions of fans. Many sports players are international celebrities. People also enjoy some very strange sports, such as underwater hockey, elephant polo, and even extreme ironing!

The Olympics in...
Ancient Greece

The first Olympic Games can be traced back to 776 BCE. This popular tournament took place in Olympia to honor the god Zeus. It was held for 12 centuries and included events such as running, wrestling, boxing, javelin, discus, and even chariot racing.

Only men were allowed to compete. Competitors didn't wear any clothes during events—they competed in the nude!

The Olympic Games were so popular that the Roman Empire found it hard to recruit men for the army during years when they were happening.

Married women were the only people not allowed to watch the games! Instead, they held their own festival, Heraia, at Olympia every four years.

The Paralympics are held after each Olympics, and showcase the sporting achievements of disabled people.

The Olympics...
Now

The Olympic Games were reintroduced in 1896. Today, they are held every four years with competitors from all over the world taking part. They have been held in 23 different countries, and it's considered a great honor to be a hosting country. The games now also include the Winter Olympics and the Paralympics.

The Olympics are far more inclusive than they were in ancient times—women have competed since 1900.

Since 2012, Muslim women have been allowed to compete in the Olympics wearing a hijab (a traditional headscarf).

Schools

Children haven't always gone to school. Formal education as we know it has only been around for a few hundred years, but children have always found ways to learn about the world. During hunter-gatherer times, they learned how to survive by exploring the land and discovering the plants and animals around them. When farming became the norm, children worked in the fields and helped to care for their growing families.

This is Sparta

Some of the earliest schools were in ancient Greece, in Sparta, and included intense military training for boys, and tough physical training for girls (so they could become strong mothers). Children began this education at around age 6 or 7 and only learned reading and writing as secondary skills.

Let Us Pray

For a long time, religious leaders were some of the only people who could read. Then, monasteries, cathedrals, and mosques opened schools to teach children so they could study the holy texts. But these schools were only open to well-off boys, while girls and poorer boys had to go to work.

A Serious Matter

Schools during the Victorian period were very strict, and punishments were common. Classes focused on hard facts in history and science, rather than creative subjects such as art and music.

Leaving Home

In much of Europe, children had to be evacuated to the countryside during the Second World War (1939-1945). During this time, many children were schooled from home, or sent to boarding schools in the countryside.

A World of Discovery

Montessori education has been around for more than 100 years, and is very different from traditional structured teaching methods. The Montessori method focuses on a child's freedom to follow their natural instincts, providing activities and environments that encourage children to learn through play. It remains popular around the world.

Going to school in...
Ancient Egypt

Schools in ancient Egypt were mostly for boys from wealthy families, but some girls did go to school and they could even become doctors and scribes. To learn the complex language of hieroglyphs, children would spend hours writing.

Boys born into poorer families learned their family's trade. Girls of lower social status would mostly learn to cook, sew, and take care of the home.

Going to school in the...
Incan Empire

In the Incan Empire of ancient Peru, school was mostly for children of nobles, but less wealthy kids would also be tested to see how intelligent they were. Those that scored the best would get to go to school too.

Both boys and girls could go to school, with girls learning skills such as weaving wool and cooking, while boys learned to read and write. They would learn stories of the empire.

Going to school during...
World War I

In the early 1900s, many schools started providing school lunches for the first time. By this time, school was mandatory for most children, so even poor children received a meal and an education.

Children didn't get out of school just because there was a war on! They still had to study and take exams.

Children today can learn all sorts of things at school, from math, English, and science, to psychology, dance, art, cooking, and music. In some Icelandic schools, kids learn to knit!

Going to school...
Now

In many countries around the world, school is mandatory for all children, so more kids than ever are getting a varied education. Schools differ greatly from place to place, and all kinds of topics are covered. Next time you are tired of homework, remember how lucky children in the past would think you are to get such an amazing education!

Getting sick

If you get sick in many parts of the world today, you can simply call a doctor or go to the hospital. People can access all kinds of medicine and treatment, even for many diseases that were once deadly. In the past, even slight infections could finish you off! For a long time, people had no idea what caused illness, and had all kinds of different theories—which led to some utterly bizarre "cures."

Herbal Remedies

With origins dating back around 2,500 years, Chinese medicine has been considered some of the most advanced throughout much of history. Herbs, massage, and acupuncture are used to cure illness, and the person as a whole is considered, rather than just the specific body part or symptom.

The Black Death

In the 1600s, a terrible plague swept Europe, killing millions of people. Its symptoms included vomiting, fever, and skin discoloration (turning black). People believed plagues were caused by bad smells, so they would carry oranges stuffed with nice-smelling spices to ward off disease. Doctors would even wear masks with strange-looking beaks, filled with spices. Today, however, the plague can be easily treated with antibiotics, a type of medicine that kills harmful bacteria.

A Trip to the Barber

Hippocrates, an ancient Greek physician, believed that disease came about when one of four "humors"—phlegm, blood, yellow bile, and black bile—was out of balance. He taught that bloodletting could correct the imbalance. As doctors were expensive, people would go to barbers to be bled—something they would sometimes do with leeches. The red-and-white striped pole outside barbershops today represents the bloody bandages used on patients. Luckily, all you'll get at a barber's today is a haircut!

The Big Chop

In the 1800s, if you badly injured a limb, it might have to come off! Surgeons would chop off arms and legs using special bone saws—often in front of a whole audience. Even worse, anesthetic wasn't invented until the 1800s, so the patient would feel the whole thing. Gruesome!

Just a Scratch

Getting a shot is never much fun, but it can save lives! The first vaccine was invented by a man called Edward Jenner, who discovered that injecting someone with a very small amount of the cowpox disease could prevent them from catching the more dangerous smallpox disease. Modern vaccines prevent all kinds of infectious diseases.

Hospitals in the...
Crimean War

When the Crimean War began in 1854, hospital conditions were atrocious, and doctors needed help. This led to the birth of modern nursing, led by women such as Florence Nightingale and Mary Seacole.

More men died from infection and disease than injuries until nurses changed the standard of care.

At first, many doctors resisted the help, but soon realized nurses could save lives.

Mary Seacole was a pioneering nurse from Jamaica. She provided amazing care for wounded soldiers, and even funded her own travel to the war zone.

Great Ormond Street Hospital in London, England, first opened its doors on Valentine's Day, 1852, with just 10 beds. It is now regarded as one of the best children's hospitals in the world.

Hospitals...
Now

Modern hospitals are usually clean, and doctors and nurses are highly trained. Today, many surgeries can be done in under an hour, and illnesses that were once lethal can be cured easily.

One day, robots controlled by doctors may be able to perform surgery!

The largest hospital in the world, in China, covers 170 acres and has 3,400 beds.

Through the years...
in Music

Music is found in every culture and country around the world, and there are many, many different types. Tribal music may have existed for 50,000 years, making it one of the most ancient art forms. People make music to express themselves, and have developed many different instruments to do so. Today, we can record and make music in more ways than ever before, using digital recording devices.

Singing, >10,000 years ago

Thousands of years ago, ancient people sang for ritual practices, to lure animals during hunts, as well as for entertainment. Many Aboriginal Australian and Native American peoples continue these traditions to this day.

Renaissance, 500 years ago

During the Renaissance, many new instruments and styles of music were created. People formed orchestras, and elaborate and often dramatic operas were performed. This era led to the popularity of great composers, including Bach and Handel.

The 1800s

The invention of the gramophone in the 1800s allowed people to record music onto a disk, which they could then listen to at home. This was revolutionary!

Ancient Persia, 6,000 years ago

Some of the earliest music can be dated back to Persia. It was played throughout religious rituals and in daily court life. Some of the earliest-known instruments originated here, such as a stringed instrument called a chang.

Medieval era, 1,200 years ago

During this period, the church was a patron of the arts and paid to train musicians. In the Bible, King David sang to God, so people saw music as a way of praying. Pope Gregory I even gave his name to a special chant, sung by monks.

Now

Today, it is possible to record and listen to music on a smartphone. Music can be made electronically, or using a huge variety of instruments, giving us more different types of music than ever before.

Music in...
Medieval times

Traveling musicians called minstrels would entertain many people, and often royal courts had their own minstrels called troubadours. They would sing songs about courtly love, far-off lands, historical events, and exciting adventures.

Minstrels played instruments that were light and easy to carry, such as the lute.

Minstrels' songs often contained continuing stories and characters, such as the tales of Robin Hood and King Arthur.

Music...
Now

Many people today enjoy live concerts, and arenas can seat thousands of people. Amplifiers and other electronics help everyone be able to hear, while amazing light shows and other specatacles are often part of the show.

New genres of music continue to emerge throughout the world. Rock, hip-hop, and pop music are some of the most popular.

First American Edition 2019
Kane Miller, A Division of EDC Publishing

Illustrated by Greg Paprocki
Written by Claire Philip

Conceived by Weldon Owen International, LLC
Copyright © 2019 Weldon Owen International, LLC
Editor: Susie Rae
Senior Designer: Emma Vince

All rights reserved. No part of this book may be reproduced,
transmitted or stored in an information retrieval system in
any form or by any means, graphic, electronic or mechanical,
including photocopying, taping or recording, without prior
written permission from the publisher.

For information, contact:
Kane Miller, A Division of EDC Publishing
PO Box 470663
Tulsa, OK 74147-0663

www.kanemiller.com
www.edcpub.com
www.usbornebooksandmore.com

Library of Congress Control Number: 2018942402

Printed in China
2 4 6 8 10 9 7 5 3 1

ISBN: 978-1-61067-863-6